I0624428

#1

# MONGREL GUN SLINGERS

## JIM LOPEZ

### "The Last Dregs of Poverty"
### Series

LSL
BOOKLETS

Published by LSL BOOKLETS
LIQUOR STORE LIT ™ is a Jim Lopez Creation
liquorstorelit.com
Los Angeles

Cover Design by Jim Lopez © 2010


ISBN-13 978-0692278956
ISBN-10 0692278958


For other works by Jim Lopez see
jimlopez.org
antiquechildren.com

# "THE LAST DREGS OF POVERTY"

### SERIES

# LSL
# BOOKLET

# MONGREL GUN SLINGERS
## JIM LOPEZ

The last time Georgia (a Yankee Doodle, donkey milking, skag-dragger) escorted a college girl (who had been featured in an episode of Girls Gone Wild and had trouble pronouncing her vowels) to an abortion he drove her to a Methodist Church, walked her up to the pulpit, made her say her prayers and then pushed her down a flight of stairs. That was a week ago, but now he and I were sitting in a cantina, listening to Corridos in Cuernavaca, Mexico.

Rumors were circulating that the Mongrel Gun Slingers had crossed the celestial border and were now themselves in Cuernavaca. It was said that they had massacred a patrol of Border Control Officers and a number of cartel members in Ciudad Juarez.

The Mongrel Gun Slingers were the Darkness in the heart of Light. They were the arm of justice, ruled by one law: justice for victims. The prayers that cried out for vengeance loosed the Mongrel Gun Slingers into this world. I didn't think much about the rumors but Georgia couldn't stop talking about the Mongrel Gun Slingers. He had some deep, disgusting desire to go out with a bang and get tag-teamed by them, and, well, Georgia was getting closer to his dream.

I shook my dick, zipped up my fly and walked back into the cantina to order another Havana *tres años* rum when I saw the Mongrel Gun Slingers for the first time. I didn't know exactly who they were, but I felt an eerie crawl down my spine as I stood next to a large woman sitting next to a large man at the bar. No one had ever lived to tell what the Mongrel Gun Slingers looked like for certain, but the few who lied dying on gurneys whispered that

the Mongrel Gun Slingers were hermaphrodites, that they were the Fifth and Sixth
Horsemen left out of the Ultimate Apocalypse
and forced to be the hand of justice in all the
'Penultimate' Apocalypses throughout the ag-
es, and no ancient scribes had dared to write
about them in public scrolls; however, I had
come across a manuscript while screwing a
Jewish girl, from Beverly Hills (who was
working on her masters at Harvard's Kennedy
School of Government), in the basement
stacks of Widner Library.

A copy of a pamphlet titled, "A Short and
Unauthorized Account of the Burning of the
Alexandrian Library" by a Bonotavio Puccini
had been rattled out the shelves and fell between my pelvic thrust and this Jewish Ameri-
can Princes' ass. It was four pages in length
and contained a drawing, which depicted the
initials MGS carved into a fallen pillar next to
the smoldering rubble of the Library of Alexandria. Supposedly, a Sumerian had cursed

Alexander the Great's general, Ptolemy I Soter, for killing his family and stealing his secret cuneiform tablets, so the Mongrel Gun Slingers crawled out of a Wormhole and sacked the Library of Alexandria.

When I mentioned the pamphlet to a Jesuit, at Weston Theological Seminary, he dismissed it as a myth, a hoax, a sort of bogyman story told to peasants by the Church to keep those who were marked for slavery illiterate and submissive. But the Mongrel Gun Slingers were no myth. They were real *Chupacabras* and I was standing right next to them.

The Mongrel Gun Slingers were the devils of the Shakin' Quakers. They were the corporeal image of Animal Magnetism. The Ouija Board would not even speak with them and when they made their presence known they were the only ones left standing.

Now what did that mean for me? Was this to be my last drink, my last few minutes of life?

Not only did the Mongrel Gun Slingers kill, but they engaged in the oldest and most feared form of warfare: they fucked their victims. Was I about to end up a raped carcass, left mutilated, and soaked in the love juice of the Hermaphroditic Fifth and Sixth Horseman, who were too vicious, brutal and obscure to be mentioned in literature?

(I had been unemployed before being unemployed was popular, and I had grown quite irritable with the fraudulent and hypocritical unemployment statistic that were spun by the United States. You see, the United States does not count everyone who is out of work; rather, it only considers those who are "eligible" for unemployment. There are more people out of work than there are those who are qualified to register for unemployment and I intended to kill someone worth killing, but the Mongrel Gun Slingers would beat me to the blade.

Jeffrey Skilling, Enron's x-CEO, as you know, had defrauded the State of California and ripped off thousands of retirement funds from hardworking Americans, and he had just been released on early parole from prison. He and his wife, Rebecca Carter, were vacationing in Cuernavaca and I wanted to kill him.)

I paid the barmaid and walked over to Georgia, placed his drink down in front of him and sat with my back towards the Mongrel Gun Slingers.

"Georgia, you see those two biggies sitting at the bar?"

"Honey, I had my eye on them since they walked in while you were tugging your pud in the alley", Georgia informed me, with his made-up queer Southern accent.

"Well, I'm not certain, but I suspect they're the Mongrel Gun Slingers."

"Really", Georgia said, leaning forward, seductively whispering and sipping his rum through a straw, "I sure hope so."

"We better get out of here."

"No, honey, we ain't goin' nowhere."

"We're sure as hell ain't going anywhere if we stay here any longer", I said with a quivering, hushed tone.

"Baby, don't worry, Georgia's here to protect-cha."

"What the fuck are talking you about, you dozy queer. They're going to kill everyone in the place. "

"Now, now Jimmy, don't exaggerate. If you've never hurt anyone so badly that he nor she pleaded to God in Precatory Prayer you'll be fine", Georgia said, eyeing the Mongrels, continuing to suck on his straw.

This overweight transvestite was flirting with the Mongrel Gun Slingers, as if he were Tennessee Williams on a bender.

"Are fucking out of your mind? Have you gone mad? Precatory! What the fuck are you talking about? We have to get out of here. Now!" I took a big swig, my heart pounding so hard I could have been impaled on a stalk of sugar cane.

Georgia had studied Patristics and Byzantine History at Gregorian University in Rome, and he received a perverted education from the priests. Now this Transvestite Princess was thinking about getting throated and crowned by these two 'mythical' lunatics. But as I mentioned before, the Mongrel Gun Slingers were no myth. They were sitting right behind me drinking Havana rum.

"Honey, didn't you study the book of Psalms in Seminary?"

"What? Yeah, I fucking did, and I know what a goddamn Precatory Psalm is. It's when some jilted fuck cries out, asking God to torture, maim and kill some vicious bastard who has it coming. But I don't give a shit. I want to get the hell out of here, now. "

"Isn't that Jeffrey Skilling and his wife, Rebecca Carter?" Georgia asked, pointing with his lips. "Didn't-cha come here to kill him?"

I turned around and sure enough there

was Skilling waving the barmaid over with a Chase Manhattan Titanium Visa Card.

"I'm going to ram that fucking Titanium card down his throat", I said forgetting the Mongrel Gun Slingers, slamming the rest of my drink.

"Go get 'em, honey. I'm here. "

The vein for murder was pumping blood so fast through my heart that I was experiencing Blind Rage for the first time. I walked up behind Skilling, grabbed his Titanium card out of his hand, pulled his head back and was about to shove my fist down his throat when I felt a hand twirl me around. It was the 'female' Mongrel staring at me with twinkling black eyes. She lifted me off my feet and sent me skidding across the floor only to be halted by the boot of the 'male' Mongrel, who heeled me right in the back of the head. "Excuse me, but this is God's business not yours", he said with a voice that resounded like a bolt of lightning thrown from the hand of Zeus. He lifted me off the floor, shoved my face in his armpit, which didn't smell as bad as I thought an Apocalyptic Horseman's pits ought to smell, and commanded, "You mustn't watch", ringing my head tighter into his armpit.

But Georgia was watching, and he gave me a blow by blow account like a queer Howard Cosell, sucking down Cuban rum with an umbrella garnish.

"The Mongrel just pulled an H&K USP .40 millimeter out her panties. I love those panties, Big Lady", Georgia said complimenting the 'female' Mongrel and then continued, "Skilling isn't looking too happy. Ooo."

I heard a bang and yanked my head out of the Mongrel's armpit. My head was bleeding into my eyes but I could see clearly. The 'female' Mongrel had stuffed the barrel of that H&K so far down Skilling's throat that she blasted his tongue and pieces of bone and various fragment of organs and tissues out of Skilling's ass, who was now lying in a lump of his own dismembered body parts, with blood and feces spilling out on the flow.

Rebecca, Skilling's wife, went screaming across the cantina. The 'male' Mongrel grabbed hold of her, bashed her head on the bar, and shoved his enormous cock right through her. He didn't even bother to raise her dress or pull down her panties before he gave her the ol' one eye. Rebecca's dress and panties wrapped around that Mongrel's member like an altar boy's lips wraps around an ice-cream cone before a priest shoves the boy's face into the cream behind the confession booth. Rebecca screamed so hard that one of her eyeballs popped out of her head. Then the Mongrel blew a load with such veracious force that it blew off the top of Rebecca's head and plastered it to the ceiling.

The 'female' Mongrel was simultaneously fucking a Federale and two of Arturo Beltrán Leyva's men (Leyva, one of Mexico's most violent drug lords, had himself been recently killed on December 16, 2009 by Mexican Special Forces, so the paper's reported). These three men had murdered the mother, the mother's son and daughter, and the mother's sister, all on the same day (December 21, 2009) that that poor mother was burying her *other* son, who was a Special Forces soldier, who had been killed during the Leyva show down. Well, now these three men were getting raped by the 'female' Mongrel, who was looking more and more like a burly Mexican dismantling a roof with a pitchfork. The Mongrel had both tools to execute the hand of justice. She was stuffing one guy's face so deep into her snatch that he started to resemble the tail of a shrimp in a taco covered in cream cheese and guacamole. That was the Federale, who was now kicking a little bit and was about to expire. The 'female' Mongrel was also giving one of Leyva's men a colonoscopy with a cock that actually roared and had teeth around its urethra. That guy was just limp and dead, while this dragon-like dick was tearing up his rectum and blowing fire through his innards. Leyva's other guy was having his dick sucked so hard that his face caved in. Then his head just disappeared into his neck, which was followed by his shoulders, chests, stomach, waist, hips, legs and feet. His whole body was sucked into his cock. Then the 'female' Mongrel chewed it up and spit it out on the wall.

Meanwhile, the 'male' Mongrel, (I describe him as 'male' even though I wasn't sure if he was a male, I mean he didn't reveal his pussy or use it to kill anyone, but after what I had just seen of the 'female' Mongrel I suspected the rumor was true—the Mongrel Gun Slingers were hermaphrodites), well, anyway, he was shooting people in the face as his cod dangled in plain view with Rebecca's other eyeball glued to the end of it. Then the 'female' Mongrel (who was half-naked) joined the 'male' Mongrel (who by the way had a double Havana rum in one hand and a John Moses

Browning commemorative .45 millimeter in the other) and started shooting people in the face as well. They killed everyone in the cantina except Georgia, me and the beautiful Mexican barmaid, who was so freighted that she jumped into my arms. I held her waiting for the Mongrel Gun Slingers to rape the two of us or shoot us both in the face. Georgia was calmly sitting at his table, gingerly and lewdly chewing his straw as he sipped his rum.

When the Mongrel's were done, so I was hoping, they walked over to the bar. The 'male' Mongrel reached over the counter, grabbed a bottle of Havana *cinco años* rum and poured two glasses. The 'female' Mongrel was composing herself in a presentable fashion. Then they lit a couple of cigarettes and peaceful drank their rum.

Georgia pursed his lips in frustrated disappointment.

"Is that all you two Herms have for us this evening", Georgia huffed like Tinker Bell pissed-off at Peter Pan. "This momentary measure of mercy better wind up with me in the arms of a *coup de main*. Are you two Mongrel Gun Slingers going to come over here and fuck me, or do I need to call a bellhop to carry my luggage up to my room?" Georgia asked with a touch of demand in his tone and a whole lot of sass.

I didn't quite understand the metaphor, but I think Georgia was looking for absolution from some past sins.

The Mongrels just sat ignoring Georgia, drinking and smoking like a couple of hard-working, unappreciated plebeians who missed happy hour. The Mexican barmaid and I were holding onto each other like a couple of huddling, uncertain characters in a Hieronymus Bosch painting.

"Ewwhoo, pppp, mmwaa, aren't you two the Mongrel Gun Slingers?" Georgia persisted, kissy-catcalling at them. "I'm ready to go to hell now."

The Mongrel Gun Slingers continued to dismiss Georgia, who was growing impatient, so he shimmied his fat ass out of his chair, sashayed across the room and leaned into the bar between both Hermaphroditic Mongrel Gun Slingers. "I said, I'm ready to get fucked and go to hell now", Georgia repeated, pouring another round of rum for himself and the Mongrels, who seemed pleased by his gesture.

The barmaid tugged herself out of my stiff arms, walked around the bar and reached for a rustic bottle of Tequila that sat on the top shelf. I followed her and sat at the end of the bar far from the Mongrels and Georgia. She placed a couple of shot glasses down between us and poured two stiff drinks. We leaned into and over the bar (the barmaid on the server's side, I on the patron's side) and stared deeply into each other's eyes, our breaths intermingling before we sucked down the cactus juice. Then she poured us another round.

"Do you know why we haven't killed you yet?" the 'male' Mongrel asked me.

The barmaid and I slammed our shots, searching for one last momentary exchange. I think I was rapidly falling in love with this green-eyed Mexican barmaid.

"We asked you a question," the 'female' Mongrel annunciated with a hallow voice that echoed.

The barmaid and I ignored the Mongrel Gun Slingers. I'd say we did so out of fright and wonder. What were the odds that Chaotic Chance would grace the two of us with romance in this bloody mess? And what did the Mongrels mean by "yet?"

"Isn't love precious," the 'male' Mongrel commented to the 'female' Mongrel.

"I want to get fucked and go to hell right now!" Georgia demanded, poking the Mongrels with his umbrella garnish. "Now, come on, do me now!" Georgia was losing his queenie composure, morphing into a spoiled child who was denied his sweets.

"No one has ever cared enough about you to consider your actions worth a damn", the 'female' Mongrel said to me. "And you little green-eyed lady, you don't get out enough", the 'male' Mongrel said to the barmaid. Then the two of them walked out of the cantina with Georgia storming after them, "You two Mongrel Gun Slingers best fuck me right now, damn-it! And I mean fuck me now! I want to go to hell!"

The barmaid and I followed them into the drizzling rain. A Wormhole opened up in the sky. The Mongrel Gun Slingers leaped in like super heroes. Georgia dove after them, head first. And the three of them disappeared. I noticed a soggy, paper rose in the gutter, so I picked it up and handed it to the barmaid. Then the two of us strolled hand-in-hand through the muddy, cracked cobbled streets, making our way to the Motel Canario. And as the clouds began to disperse the crescent moon appeared, shining bright in the black sky and we could hear, in the distant yet ever-so-close parallel universe, Georgia–not whistling Dixie but–nagging, "I want to get fucked and go to hell, right now!"